Lo que aprendo / The Things I Learn

Aprendo de abuelito
I Learn from My Grandpa

Lorraine Harrison

traducido por / translated by Charlotte Bockman

ilustrado por / illustrated by
Anita Morra

PowerKiDS press.

New York

Published in 2018 by The Rosen Publishing Group, Inc.
29 East 21st Street, New York, NY 10010

First Edition

Translator: Charlotte Bockman
Editorial Director, Spanish: Nathalie Beullens-Maoui
Editor, Spanish: Rossana Zúñiga
Editor, English: Greg Roza
Art Director: Michael Flynn
Book Design: Raúl Rodriguez
Illustrator: Anita Morra

Cataloging-in-Publication Data

Names: Harrison, Lorraine.
Title: I learn from my grandpa = Aprendo de abuelito / Lorraine Harrison.
Description: New York : PowerKids Press, 2018. | Series: The things I learn = Lo que aprendo | In English and Spanish. Includes index.
Identifiers: ISBN 9781508163725 (library bound)
Subjects: LCSH: Grandfathers–Juvenile literature. | Grandparent and child–Juvenile literature.
Classification: LCC HQ759.9 H383 2018 | DDC 306.874'5–dc23

Manufactured in the United States of America

CPSIA Compliance Information: Batch #BW18PK. For further information contact Rosen Publishing, New York, New York at 1-800-237-9932

Contenido

Vamos a hacer algo	4
Pintando con mi abuelito	14
Es hora de limpiar	20
Palabras que debes aprender	24
Índice	24

Contents

Let's Make Something	4
Painting with Grandpa	14
Time to Clean Up	20
Words to Know	24
Index	24

Me gusta estar con mi abuelito.
Me enseña muchas cosas nuevas.

I love being with my grandpa.
He teaches me lots of new things.

A mi abuelito le gusta hacer cosas.

My grandpa likes to make things.

¡También me enseña cómo hacer cosas!

He teaches me to make things too!

Vamos a hacer
una cometa.

We're going to
make a kite.

Necesitamos dos palos, papel y cuerda.

We need two sticks, paper, and some string.

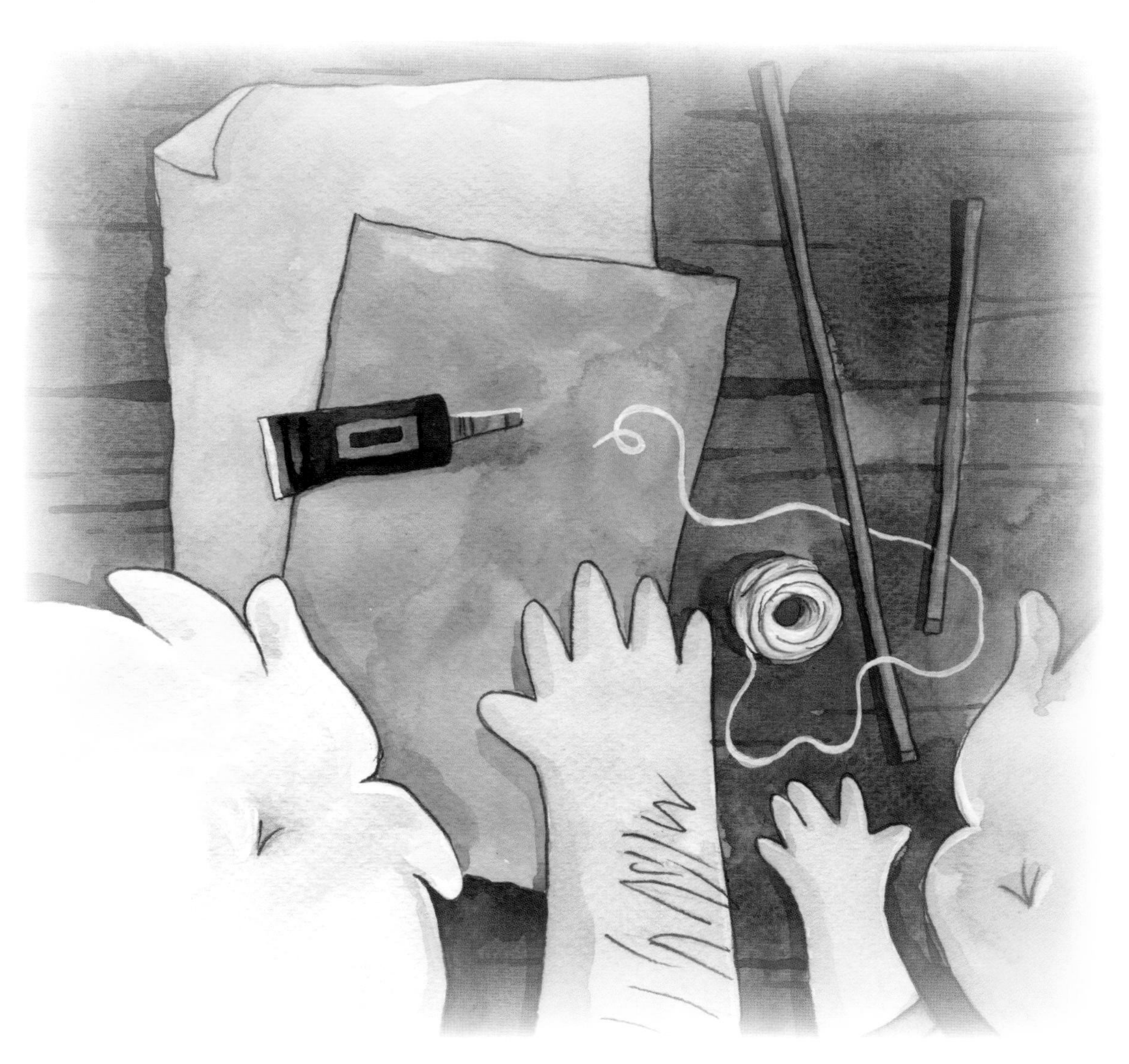

Abuelito me enseña cómo volar la cometa.

El viento hace que vuele alto.

Grandpa teaches me how to fly the kite.

The wind helps it go high.

Empieza a llover.

It starts to rain.

Mi abuelito dice que la lluvia viene de las nubes.

My grandpa says rain comes from clouds.

A mi abuelito y a mí nos gusta pintar.
Hacemos un dibujo juntos.

Grandpa and I like to paint.
We paint a picture together.

Hacemos un dibujo de la casa de mi abuelito.

We paint a picture of Grandpa's house.

Aprendo a mezclar
los colores.

I learn how to mix
colors together.

Hicimos un bonito dibujo.

We made a pretty picture.

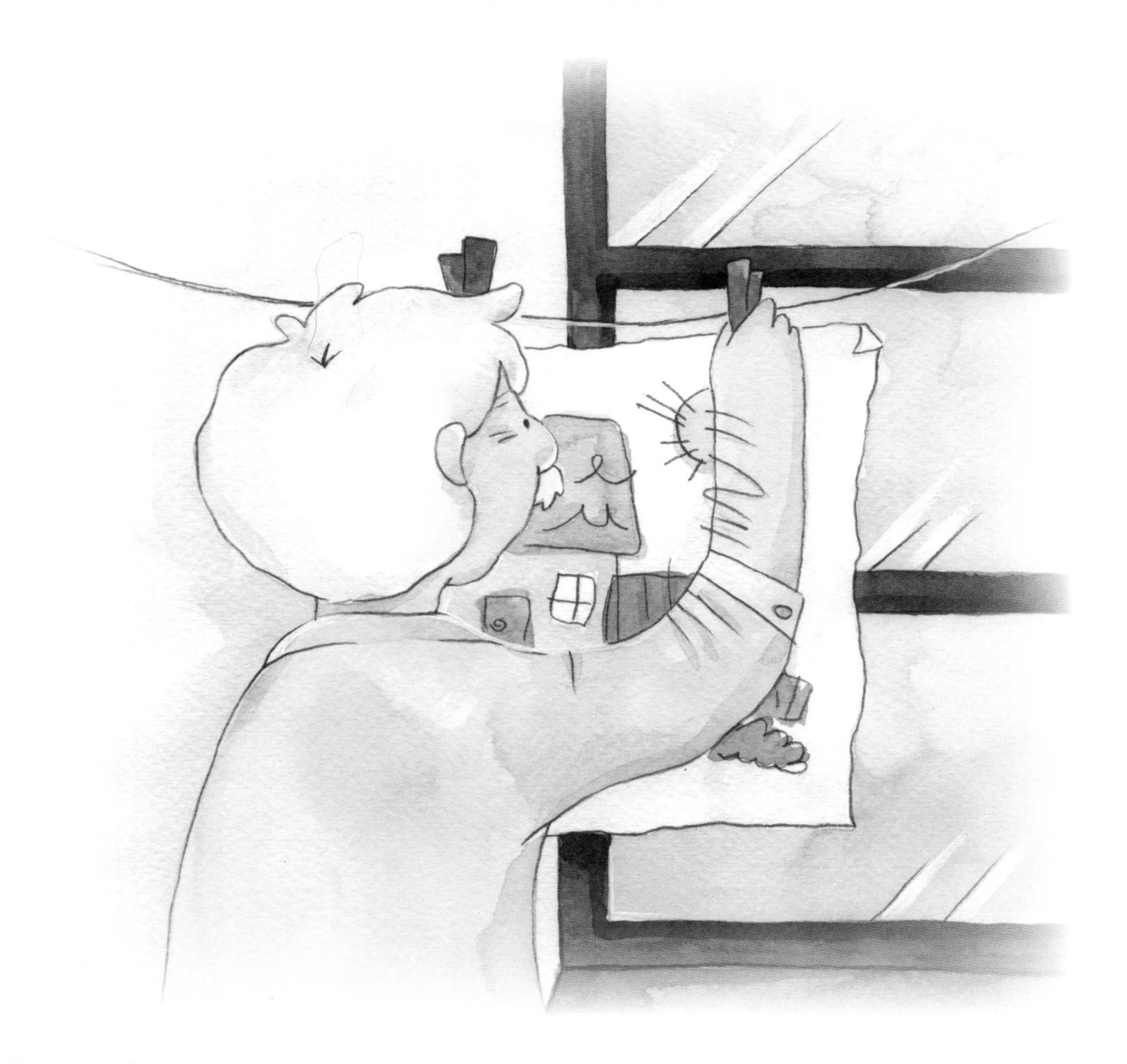

Lo dejamos cerca de la ventana para que se seque.

We let it dry near the window.

La mesa está toda desordenada.

The table's a mess.

Abuelito me enseña cómo limpiar.

My grandpa teaches me how to clean up.

¡Mi abuelito es el mejor maestro!

My grandpa is the best teacher!

Palabras que debes aprender
Words to Know

(el) desorden
mess

(la) lluvia
rain

(la) ventana
window

Índice / Index

C

cometa / kite, 8, 11

E

enseñar / teaches, 4, 7, 11, 21

L

lluvia / rain, 12, 13

P

pintura / paint, 15, 16

DISCARDED BY
FREEPORT
MEMORIAL LIBRARY